Everything he did, Small Bunny
did with Blue Blanket.

Small Bunny needed Blue Blanket to help him go even higher on the swings.

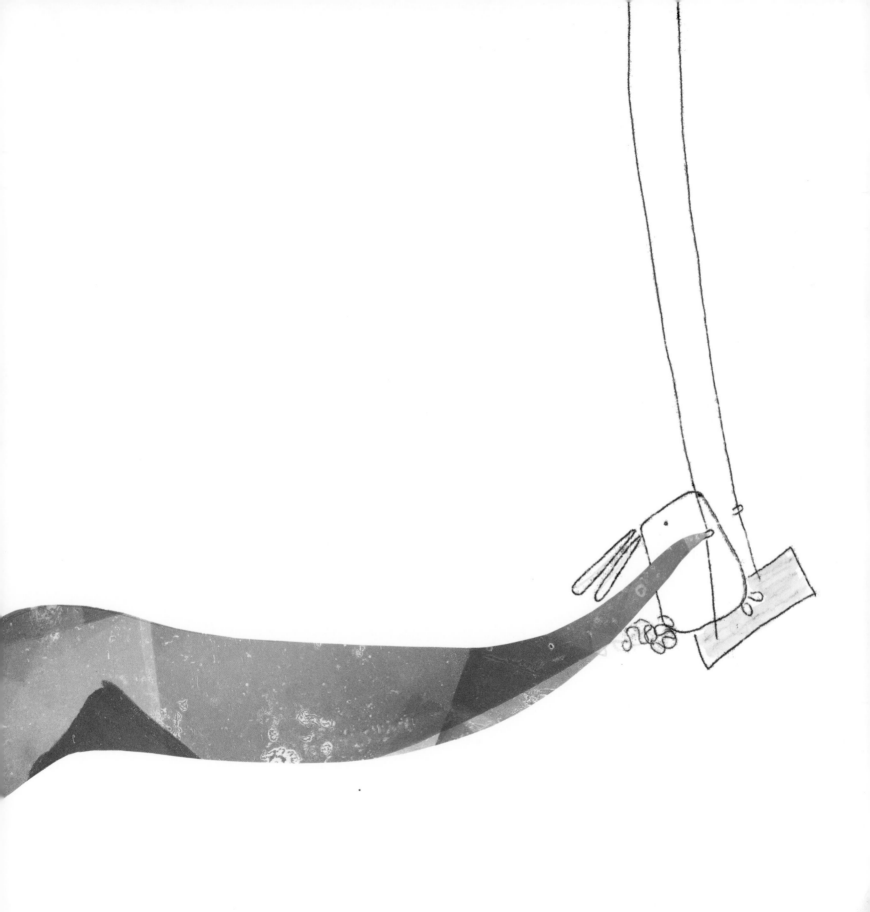

He needed Blue Blanket
to help him paint
his best pictures . . .

and he needed Blue Blanket
to help him read the hardest
words in his books.

Small Bunny and Blue Blanket
were always together.

One day, when they
were in the sandpit . . .

Mummy called, 'Time to come in
Small Bunny, you both need a wash.'

Small Bunny thought Blue Blanket
was perfect the way it was.

His Mummy didn't agree.

'Bunny!'

After Small Bunny was washed . . .

and dried . . .

. . . Mummy picked up Blue Blanket and put it in the washing machine.

'Don't worry,' she said,
'it will only take a minute.'

It actually took 107.

And Small Bunny watched
Blue Blanket for every single one.

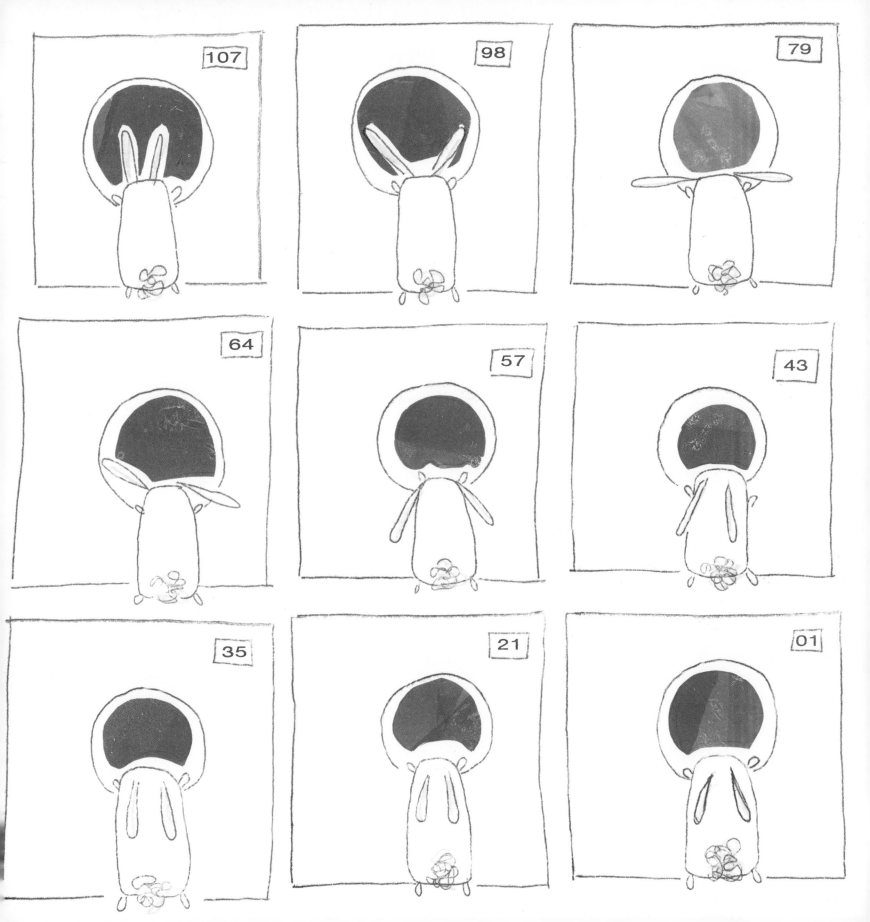

Mummy hung Blue Blanket out to dry.

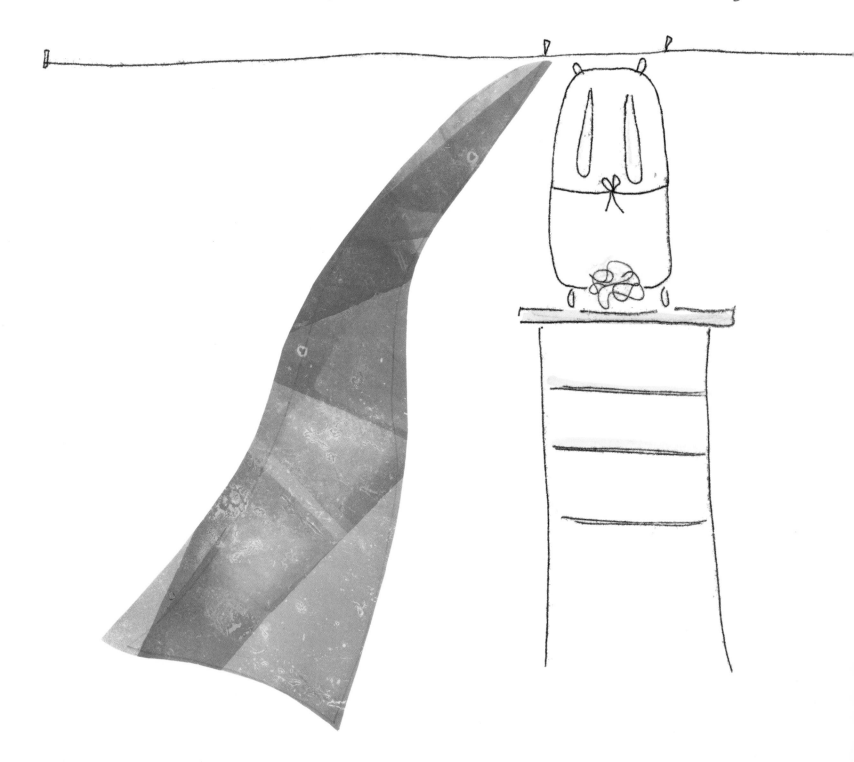

'Good as new!' she said.

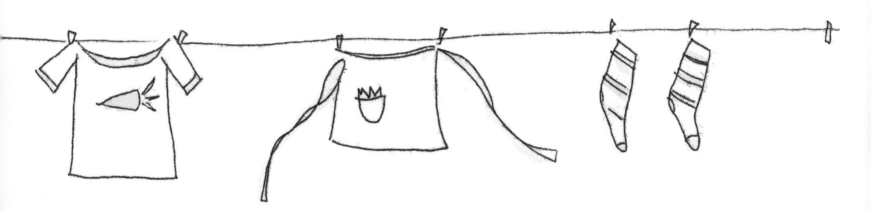

Small Bunny did not agree.

He did not like new.

But after plenty of swinging,

painting,

reading,

and playing . . .

. . . Blue Blanket was
just the way it was before.

Perfect.

To my Mom and Dad

OXFORD
UNIVERSITY PRESS

Great Clarendon Street, Oxford OX2 6DP

Oxford University Press is a department of the University of Oxford.
It furthers the University's objective of excellence in research, scholarship,
and education by publishing worldwide in

Oxford   New York

Auckland Cape Town Dar es Salaam Hong Kong Karachi
Kuala Lumpur Madrid Melbourne Mexico City Nairobi
New Delhi Shanghai Taipei Toronto

With offices in

Argentina Austria Brazil Chile Czech Republic France Greece
Guatemala Hungary Italy Japan Poland Portugal Singapore
South Korea Switzerland Thailand Turkey Ukraine Vietnam

Oxford is a registered trade mark of Oxford University Press
in the UK and in certain other countries

Text and illustrations © Tatyana Feeney 2012

The moral rights of the author/illustrator have been asserted

Database right Oxford University Press (maker)

First published in 2012

British Library Cataloguing in Publication Data available

ISBN: 978-0-19-275792-0 (hardback)
ISBN: 978-0-19-275793-7 (paperback)

2 4 6 8 10 9 7 5 3 1

Printed in China

Paper used in the production of this book is a natural,
recyclable product made from wood grown in sustainable forests.
The manufacturing process conforms to the environmental
regulations of the country of origin